DIRECTOR'S CUT

THE ATLAS OF CURSED PLACES

DIRECTOR'S CUT

VANESSA ACTON

MINNEAPOLIS

Darby Creek
A division of Lerner Publishing Group, Inc.
241 First Avenue North
Minneapolis, MN 55401 USA

For reading levels and more information, look up this title at www.lernerbooks.com.

The images in this book are used with the permission of: © iStockphoto.com/pboehringer (houses); © iStockphoto.com/Jürgen François (ghosts); © iStockphoto.com/mustafahacalaki (skull); © iStockphoto.com/Igor Zhuravlov (storm); © iStockphoto.com/desifoto (graph paper); © iStockphoto.com/Trifonenko (blue flame); © iStockphoto.com/Anita Stizzoli (dark clouds).

Main body text set in Janson Text LT Std 12/17.5.
Typeface provided by Adobe Systems.

Library of Congress Cataloging-in-Publication Data
The Cataloging-in-Publication Data for *Director's Cut* is on file at the Library of Congress.
ISBN 978-1-5124-1324-3 (lib. bdg.)
ISBN 978-1-5124-1351-9 (pbk.)
ISBN 978-1-5124-1352-6 (EB pdf)

Manufactured in the United States of America
1-39783-21321-3/18/2016

For A.H. May you never be abandoned in a corn maze.

CHAPTER 1

This isn't the worst idea I've ever had.

My friend Ahmed would probably disagree. But only because he hasn't known me that long. "We shouldn't be here," he says.

If it were up to him, I think we'd never leave the base. And yeah, Edmonds Air Force Base is a great place to live. Bowling alley, pool, gym, movie theater, park. Endless bike-friendly streets.

But seriously. An abandoned movie set trumps all of that.

"It's fine," I tell him. The four of us—Ahmed, Destiny, Gabby, and me—stand in a line, straddling our bikes. We're all staring at the fence. Or at least Ahmed and I are. Destiny and Gabby are probably straining to see what's *beyond* the fence. The distant outlines of deserted buildings. The sun in our eyes doesn't help.

We can see the fence just fine, though. It's taller than I expected. Maybe twenty feet. But it's just an ordinary chain-link deal. No barbed wire. No electricity. No fancy security, like the base has. And why would there be? There's nothing here worth protecting. Sanford's Folly is just a ghost town. A *fake* ghost town. An old, forgotten movie set that's been closed for thirty years. Out in the middle of the Arizona desert. Barely within sight of the one road that runs past it. Nobody will know or care if we sneak in. Sure, there's a NO TRESPASSING sign. But it's old and worn-out looking, hanging slightly crooked. It clearly doesn't take itself seriously anymore.

Ahmed shakes his head. "I'm just getting a really bad feeling about this."

Gabby lets out an irritated grunt. "Thanks, Han Solo." She never misses a chance to make a movie reference. Usually she goes for something way more obscure than *Star Wars*. Gabby's what you would call a film nerd. Which is why she's here. Destiny came along because she loves a good case of paranormal activity. She's heard the rumors about Sanford's Folly and wants to see if they're true. Me, I'm just in it for a change of routine. And Ahmed . . . well . . .

"You didn't have to come," I tell him. Which isn't fair. I mean, it's true. He *didn't*. But I know he was afraid to turn down the invitation. Afraid I'd judge him. Afraid I wouldn't want to hang out with him anymore. He and his family have been at Edmonds way longer than Mom and I have. Almost a year. But he didn't have a core group of friends here until this past month, when I brought the four of us together. Gabby and Destiny definitely didn't hang out with him before. So I know he's feeling the pressure.

I've been there. I know it's a gut-eating feeling. Even worse, in a way, than being totally alone. And I've been there too. "It's fine if you want to go back," I add. "Or if you just want to wait here with the bikes. For real, man. But I'm doing this."

"So am I," says Destiny. Like anyone was in doubt. Her silver charm bracelet slides down her arm as she lifts her hand to wipe the sweat off her forehead.

"I'll go first," declares Gabby. She lets go of her bike, which slumps sideways into the sand. By the time I engage my own bike's kickstand, she's climbed halfway up the fence.

"But what if it really is . . ." Ahmed trails off.

"Cursed?" Destiny finishes for him. She takes a last swig from her water bottle and settles it back in the basket between her bike's handlebars. The little charms on her bracelet clink together like mini wind chimes. Minus the wind. The desert air is dead still. "That's what we're here to find out. Whether it's cursed or not."

This is why they wouldn't be hanging out if it weren't for me. Destiny thinks the idea of a curse is cool. Ahmed, not so much.

Still, Ahmed follows the rest of us to the fence. I grab a handhold between the metal links and start hoisting myself up. Destiny and Ahmed are right behind me. In two seconds, Destiny passes me. She almost overtakes Gabby, who's swinging a leg over the top of the fence. I suspect she let Gabby get a head start just so she could outpace her. They have that kind of half-respect, half-rivalry thing going on.

A few seconds later I reach the top. The fence sways a little under our combined weight. Up here, that swaying feels more dramatic. I sneak a glance back over my shoulder. Our bikes wait in a cluster. Beyond them, there's nothing but sand all the way to the horizon. The road isn't far away, but I can't see it from here. The late afternoon sun is at that mellow point before sunset kicks in.

I face forward again and swing my right leg over the fence. Once I find a new foothold on the other side, I bring my other leg over. Below me, I hear Gabby's feet hit the ground. Then Destiny's.

Mom would kill me if she knew about this. I try to ignore that thought. Mom isn't some military stereotype, barking orders at home, saying things like "I want your room clean by Oh-Eight-Hundred-Hours." She's actually pretty chill. Except when I, well, break the law.

Soon I'm on the ground. Ahmed lands next to me. We all start walking. Sanford's Folly comes clearly into view.

Like I said, it's a fake town, built in the 1930s to look like an old-style frontier settlement. Lots of famous cowboy movies got filmed here. Gabby can probably name most of them, even though she hates Westerns.

Now, though, the place looks like a construction site that got hit by a tornado. A few crumbling stone buildings line each side of the wide "main street," which is really just a bare stretch of packed sand. The street eventually dead-ends in front of a big, whiteish stone building with a peaked roof. There's an empty space where its front door used to be. From here, it looks as if that doorway is staring us down. Daring us to walk all the way up to it.

"All the way" isn't actually very far. The whole stretch of the town is only as long as a football field, tops. But we're taking our time, shuffling past the wrecked structures. Destiny keeps pausing to snap pictures with her phone.

Every so often there's a pile of rubble where a wooden building used to be. Charred, rotting timber. Two or three sagging walls guarding a gutted foundation. Caved-in ceilings. Window frames full of sky. Glinting fragments of metal buried in the wreckage.

Random things stand out to me. A jagged piece of a sign with the letters *SHER* still readable under the scorch marks. A soot-blackened metal pot—I think it's called a spittoon. Half of a saloon door.

"When was the fire?" I ask Gabby. "The one that shut the place down for good?"

I don't know why I'm whispering.

"Eighties," Gabby whispers back. She dodges a tumbleweed that rolls into her path.

"That's what I thought. Weird that they never, like, cleaned up afterward."

Gabby shrugs. "The studio probably didn't want to spend the money for that. The guys in charge decided right away that they wouldn't film here again."

"Yeah," says Destiny. "Since the fire pretty much clinched the whole 'curse' thing."

"Nothing *clinched* the curse thing," says Gabby, rolling her eyes. "There just happened to be plenty of other movie sets. And Westerns were getting less popular by then anyway. Fixing up this place wouldn't have been worth the trouble."

Another knotted ball of tumbleweed blows past us. Weird. There's not any wind right now. What's making it move?

"What *is* the curse, exactly?" I ask. "I mean, supposedly." I've only heard the vague rumors that a curse exists.

"Eternal bad luck for all who enter here," says Destiny over her shoulder. Casually, like she's telling me the time.

Gabby makes a dismissive noise in her throat. "Yeah. Nothing *specific*. Nothing you can actually measure or prove. Convenient, right?"

Destiny steps closer to a collapsed building. She climbs over the closest layer of stone chunks and warped wooden planks. "Let's check out some of the side streets," she says, pointing like an explorer in a textbook.

"But Main Street was where they did all the filming," protests Gabby.

"So what are the other buildings for?" I ask.

Gabby shrugs. "Eating. Applying the actors' makeup. Storing the costumes and props and film equipment. All very important. Just not as interesting as the actual film set."

More tumbleweeds gather around us. Three, four, five of these feather-light, dried-up plants. This time they don't seem to be just blowing by. They roll to a stop and sit there. Like they're watching us.

The others haven't noticed. "Come on," says Destiny. She's already scrabbling deeper into the mess of the demolished building. Never mind that we could easily cut *between* buildings to get to a parallel street. Destiny loves a challenge. "Isn't the behind-the-scenes stuff the most interesting part anyway?"

"Sure, when it hasn't all burned to a crisp," says Gabby. "But it's not like there'll be a bunch of old costumes or props to discover. They cleared out anything they could salvage years ago. Besides, I want to see the mission." She points toward the far end of the street. The whitish building. A mission, huh? I guess it does look kind of like a church. That peak at the top must be the bell tower.

"Yeah, let's finish our tour of Main Street first," I say.

"Feel free," says Destiny. She's reached the back end of the building's foundation. She steps over the last clump of broken-up stone. "You can meet me when you're done. I'll be over this way."

I'm not an expert like Gabby, but I've seen enough horror movies to know splitting up is a bad idea. "Um, are you sure . . .?"

Destiny glances back now. "You're not *scared*, are you, Alex?"

"No, I just . . ."

I glance around and realize the tumbleweeds have disappeared. I must be losing it. Thinking that tumbleweeds are stalking us.

"Look, guys, I gotta be back by sunset," Ahmed says. Sunset is one of his prayer times.

"Don't worry," Gabby tells him. "It only took forty minutes to bike here. If we leave by . . ." She pauses to check her phone. "If we leave by five, we're fine."

She grabs me by the arm and drags me toward the adobe building. Ahmed follows us.

"Maybe I should go with Destiny," I say. I don't like the idea of her wandering off alone. Andrea Milton never forgave me for ditching her in that corn maze in fourth grade.

"Or maybe you should chill out," says Gabby. "Destiny can take care of herself."

About five seconds later, we hear Destiny scream.

CHAPTER 2

We take off running, following Destiny's voice.

We cut between two buildings and come out on the next street. Here, we see more fire-hollowed structures. No obvious sign of Destiny.

We're yelling her name and "Where are you?" But she's not answering. Gabby tries calling her. Straight to voicemail.

"She couldn't have gone far," said Ahmed. "Where's the spot where she crossed over? Back there, right? So let's check the buildings closest to that spot."

Something I didn't know about Ahmed until this moment: he's good in a crisis.

"We stay together, though," I insist.

"Agreed," says Gabby. Then she starts shouting "Destiny!" again.

We go from building shell to building shell. These buildings are more modern than the ones on Main Street. But they're in even worse shape. In the fourth place we check, there's a massive hole in the middle of the floor.

"Destiny?" I call out like it's a question. I can't make myself go near the hole. This was all my idea. If she's hurt, it's my fault. Gabby steps up to the hole and peers in. Shakes her head. "Nothing down there except bits of the floor that fell in."

"Hold on. *Something* has to be down there," says Ahmed. "Or the floor wouldn't have caved in. It wouldn't have had anything to cave in *on.*"

Gabby looks back down into the hole. "Yeah, well, I guess it's some kind of basement. But it's empty. She's not there."

I finally work up the guts to crouch down next to the hole and look in. Gabby's right. Except . . .

Among the fragments of plaster flooring, I spot a tiny glimmer of silver.

"Her bracelet's down there," I say. "Her charm bracelet." My voice comes out scratchy and deep.

Gabby swears softly. She dials her phone again. Under her breath she mutters, "Come on, come on, pick *up* . . ."

"Maybe we should call 9-1-1," says Ahmed.

I have a different idea. I sit down and let my legs hang over the edge of the hole.

Gabby lowers her phone. "What are you—"

"Alex," says Ahmed. "No. No way, man."

"That basement is bigger than what we can see through the hole," I say. "She could be down there, out of our line of sight. She could be unconscious."

"Can we not assume the worst?" Gabby says. "She might be fine."

Then why isn't she answering her phone? Why didn't she respond when we shouted her name? I don't insult Gabby by saying any of that. I just go with, "We have to check."

"You are not going down there," Ahmed says sternly.

"It can't be much more than a ten-foot drop from here," I say. Like that's not far enough to break any bones if I land wrong.

"And how are you planning to get back up?" demands Ahmed. "We don't have a rope."

"I bet you could find a pole or a metal bar or something," I say. "Or I guess you could call 9-1-1 at that point." If I find Destiny down there, injured, he'll have to do that anyway.

Before either of them can stop me, I drop down. It's not the smartest way to go. I could've faced the other way and lowered myself more slowly, dangled by my hands. But I'm in a hurry.

I land hard but not too hard. I snatch up Destiny's bracelet and look around. It's dark. I pull out my phone and shine it in front of me, first on the ground. I'm holding my breath, terrified I'll see Destiny's crumpled body on the floor. I don't. For a second I'm relieved. Until I think, *But if she's not here, where . . . ?*

That's when I see it.

"Uh, guys . . ."

"What?" asks Gabby. She and Ahmed are down on their knees, leaning over the edge of the hole.

"There's an opening in the wall down here. It looks like . . ."

I take a few steps closer. Shine my phone light into the darkness. Yeah. Definitely.

"Looks like *what*?" barks Gabby.

"A tunnel."

CHAPTER 3

We know it's a bad idea for all three of us to jump through the hole into the basement and follow this tunnel. But Gabby doesn't want me going alone. And Ahmed doesn't want to be left behind by himself.

So now we're all walking through the tunnel. Our phones offer some feeble light, but we can't see very far in front of us. I keep my free hand pressed to the cold clay wall, feel my way along.

"I wonder if this was the tunnel Earl Morrison used to meet up with Simone DeVray," whispers Gabby.

"Who and who?" I say.

"Earl Morrison. Western movie mega-star? He filmed, like, six or seven movies at Sanford's Folly. And he costarred with this actress named Simone DeVray a few times. And they had this big affair."

One good thing about movie trivia: it helps you forget that one of your friends is missing.

"Why wouldn't they just meet up in their trailers?" I ask.

"A guy like Earl Morrison didn't have a *trailer*," sniffs Gabby. "He rented entire hotels. He had whole buildings set aside for him on studio lots. Rumor had it that he liked to have secret tunnels built on movie sets, so that he could go places without being followed and watched by a zillion people. He was a huge deal, back in the thirties and forties and fifties and—"

"Got it," I said. "Well, I don't know about him, but if *I* had to use a creepy tunnel like this to meet up with my lady friend, it would kinda kill the mood."

Suddenly a wall looms up in front of us. But there's a doorway cut into the wall. Wait, not a doorway.

"A staircase," breathes Gabby.

That's an exaggeration. It's more like a wheelchair ramp with a few token ridges cut into it. But at the top, there's a wooden trapdoor that I push open.

Above us, there's another shriek.

"Destiny?" I yelp.

I stick my head up through the opening and see several things at once. Four wooden walls. Some smallish metal cylinders stacked on the wooden floor.

And Destiny, staring down at me, a hand over her mouth. "Oh, hey, Alex. Scared me."

"*We* scared *you*?" I launch myself into the room. It seems to be some kind of shed. Mostly empty, with plenty of room for the four of us. "Why didn't you answer when we were yelling for you?"

She looks surprised. "I didn't hear any yelling."

Gabby and Ahmed climb up behind me.

"I tried calling you!" Gabby snaps at her.

"You did?" Destiny pulls out her phone to

check. "It didn't buzz . . . You tried to call me *eight times*?"

"We heard you scream," says Ahmed. "We thought you were hurt."

"Oh, yeah." Destiny shrugs. "I fell through the floor in one of the other buildings. But I guess you figured that out. Isn't the tunnel cool?"

"So you're okay," I say. I'm almost more irritated than relieved.

"Yeah," she chirps.

I shove her bracelet at her. "Here. You dropped this."

"Oh, thanks! My dad gave that to me. Can't believe I let it fall off." As she takes it, she gives me a weird look. Probably because I'm glaring at her. "What's up with you?"

"Nothing. Just that you *disappeared*."

"Well, I'm fine. No harm done, right?"

I can't argue with that. She wasn't playing some kind of trick on us, worrying us on purpose. I don't have a good excuse to be annoyed at her. I just don't like losing track of people.

She's already moved on. "Check this out." She picks up one of the metal cylinders. "Gabby, aren't these, like, old-school film reels?" She splits the cylinder in half, and I realize it's actually a container. Now that she's lifted the lid, we can see what's inside.

"Looks like a mini tire," I say, looking at the wheel-shaped metal object nestled in the case.

"Well, it's not," says Gabby dryly. Then her tone shifts gears, lifting with excitement. "You're right, Destiny. It's a film reel. Thirty-five-millimeter, I bet." She gently lifts it out of the case. I catch a glimpse of a dark, translucent ribbon wrapped around the reel's edge.

"Is that the actual film?" I ask, pointing. I like knowing how stuff works, how different parts fit together. That's how I got good with computers.

Gabby sighs. I can tell she doesn't consider me a budding film guru. "Yes, Alex. It's called a print." She carefully turns the reel over in her hands. Destiny starts looking through the other stacks. I join her. Some of the reels have labels. I read them even though they don't make much sense.

Hard Trail, Morrison promo.

Bride of the West, Trailer.

Willis screen test.

MWTSS.

BOTW, Morrison interview . . .

The alarm on Ahmed's phone goes off.

"Is it five already?" asks Gabby.

"Almost," says Ahmed.

"Oh, sorry, man," I say. "We'd better get going."

Gabby and Destiny package up the reel again and put it back with the stack.

When we step out of the shed, I realize we're at the far edge of Sanford's Folly. This wooden shed sits by itself on the outskirts of the town. We're at least fifty yards away from the white building, the mission. I glance in the opposite direction, away from the town. Nothing but more sand, a few scraggly cacti, and the surrounding metal fence.

I take another look at the shed. Up until now, we haven't seen any intact wooden buildings here. But this one—it looks like the fire never even winked at it. Huh.

"Earth to Alex," says Gabby. "Ahmed's not the only one who has stuff to do tonight. Can we pick up the pace?"

We're skirting around the mission and stepping back onto Main Street when we see the coyote.

It's standing in the middle of the street, facing us. Blocking our path.

We all freeze. "Just back up slowly," whispers Destiny. "They don't usually attack people."

"Unless they're rabid," mutters Ahmed.

I had no idea either of them knew anything about coyotes. But hey, I'm not complaining.

"It doesn't look rabid," I say.

That's when it charges at us.

"New plan," says Destiny. "Run."

CHAPTER 4

We veer to the right and duck over to the next street. As we sprint up that street, I gasp, "How'd it even get in here?"

"Must be a hole in the fence somewhere," Ahmed pants.

The coyote dashes out in front of us— closer now. And it's not alone this time. Two more—three more?—come barreling onto the street from both sides.

"Split up!" shouts Ahmed.

This time I don't argue with that idea.

Ahmed turns around and doubles back. Gabby goes right. Destiny and I go left. Back to Main Street.

I can hear the coyotes growling as they chase us.

Destiny dashes straight across Main Street and keeps going, disappearing onto another side street. I head straight up the main drag. Well, not quite straight. I do the snake run, weaving back and forth in a sharp zigzag. Which might be the only reason I don't get tackled by a coyote. Because I can hear one right behind me, jaws snapping. Not quite catching anything in its teeth. Yet.

But it's going to catch me any second now. I'm a sprinter on the track team, but I'm not exactly an Olympic prospect. These animals can outrun *deer*. And then they, you know, *disembowel* said deer.

And now there's another one in front of me. I don't have time to figure out where it came from. I just know that I'm about three feet away from a mauling.

Attack by rabid coyote is not on my list of Top Ten Ways I'm Willing to Die.

I swerve to the side, through the empty doorway of a roofless stone building. The walls are about eight feet high. But the empty window frames are set pretty low. Low enough for me to hoist myself up onto a window ledge.

From there I easily boost myself onto the top of the wall. A coyote leaps up right behind me and nips the heel of my shoe just before I scramble all the way up. That's as high as it can jump, though. The two coyotes take turns lunging at me. They both fall about a foot short.

But my balance on top of this wall is iffy. The stone blocks are just slightly wider than one of my feet. I'm crouched down, gripping the wall with my hands to stay in place. I'm about to jump down to the other side of the wall when I see the third coyote waiting there. "How many of you *are* there?" Then I look around for another exit.

The building right next to this one is also made of stone. Also with no roof. But much taller. Or at least some of it is. Looks like it used to be two stories. The wall facing me has partly collapsed. It's maybe five feet higher than the top of my wall. Eye level with me, if I were standing up straight.

I try to guess the distance between the two buildings. Probably not more than eight feet. Definitely not more than ten. I hope.

Because if this doesn't work, I'm dead. Or at least badly tooth-marked.

I turn my body as best I can. And leap.

Half a second later, I open my eyes. My arms are hooked over the top of the other building's wall. The rest of my body flops below me. Success. Sort of. Now I'm fifteen-ish feet off the ground. Still in the crosshairs of at least one coyote. With even less of an exit strategy than before.

And now the stone wall I'm clinging to is starting to vibrate.

Just little tremors at first. I'm not sure if it's just my own shaking, the pounding of my own heart. But now I feel the shaking get stronger. Shudders running through the stone itself.

This wall's about to come down.

It seems to happen in slow motion. The wall tips sideways, toward what used to be the inside of the building. I can't tell if it's tipping over as a complete package, like a Lego tower, or if different sections of it are buckling and breaking up into separate chunks of stone. All I'm sure of is that I'm about to hit the ground. Ground that's already strewn with rubble.

Maybe death by coyote wasn't my worst option after all.

CHAPTER 5

I seem to be alive. I'm choking on dust and my whole body hurts. But I'm already stumbling to my feet and breaking into a run.

I'm running blindly. I think I'm out on Main Street again. Yeah, there's the fence up ahead. Are the coyotes still chasing me? I can't tell. I don't hear them. Maybe the wall's collapse scared them off.

Maybe I've gone deaf.

No, I can hear Destiny shouting up ahead.

I'm at the fence. Finally. I climb. My legs ache. My shoulders burn. But I climb. Up, over, and down.

I collapse in the sand and gulp big breaths. Safe.

After a few seconds I raise my head and look around. No sign of the coyotes on the other side of the fence. It's almost like they vanished into thin air.

Gabby's bent over, hands on her knees, breathing hard. Ahmed is kneeling next to Destiny, who sits cradling her left arm.

"You guys okay?" I wheeze.

Destiny winces. "I fell on the way down the fence."

Destiny fell? *Destiny*, the best climber of the four of us?

"Is your arm . . .?"

"I can't tell. Hurts a lot."

I flash back to three years ago, when Ryan Daniels fell off my roof while we were playing extreme Ultimate Frisbee. Broke his ankle. I promised my mom I'd never try something that stupid again.

"Will you be able to ride your bike?"

She manages to snort. "Of course. You think only guys can do those no-hands stunts?"

I laugh shakily. Ahmed goes to my bike, grabs my water bottle out of the holder at the back, and brings it to me. "Thanks," I say. I take a long swig, then look back at the fence. "How many coyotes do you think there were?"

"Too many," Destiny pants. "Coyotes hardly ever travel in packs. Pairs at the most. And they hardly ever attack humans. I did a whole report on them last spring. What happened back there was *not* normal."

"Don't start with the stupid curse stuff," Gabby snaps.

"Do you have another explanation?" Destiny fires back. "They didn't even seem rabid. Did they?"

"I wouldn't know! I don't have a college degree in animal behavior. And guess what? Neither do you."

If you want to strain a friendship that's only a few weeks old, throw a coyote attack into the mix. These two are at their limit, I can tell.

"Okay," I say, pushing myself to my feet. "We need to get out of here."

Once we're back on the road, we pedal like our lives depend on it. Ahmed's out in front. Destiny's right behind him—one arm tucked against her chest, the other gripping a handlebar. The key is momentum, I guess. I just hope Ahmed doesn't have to brake suddenly.

We make it back to base just as the last sliver of the sun kisses the horizon. At the front gate, we half-fall off our bikes and fumble for our military ID cards. Ahmed shows his card to the checkpoint guard. Then he waves to us, jumps back on his bike, and takes off. I hope he makes it to his apartment in time for his sunset prayer.

I reach into my jeans pocket for my wallet. It's not there.

Gabby and Destiny have both shown their IDs. They look back at me, waiting.

"I—I think I lost my wallet," I stutter. I look at the poker-faced checkpoint guard. "My ID card was in there. But my name's Alex Ventura, and my mom is Staff Sergeant Claudia Ventura."

"Can't let you in without an ID card or a visitor pass," he says gruffly.

I spend the next fifteen minutes trying to talk my way into a high-security Air Force base. I give the guy my full name, my social-security number, the name of my mom's commanding officer, and a summary of her career history. And when none of that works, I call my mom.

Now she really *is* going to kill me.

***

"*What* did you do?"

Those are Mom's first words to me after she gets me past the checkpoint. She finally convinced the guard to let me through by showing him my birth certificate, my social-security card, and a scanned copy of my military ID card. Good thing she's the type of person who keeps that kind of stuff on hand.

I load my bike into the backseat of Mom's car. It's a good way to avoid her question.

"*Alex,*" she says.

"It's a long story, Mom."

"Does it have anything to do with those cuts and bruises?"

I was hoping it would be too dark for her to see how scraped up I am. "I fell off my bike earlier. My wallet must've slipped out of my pocket then."

Not a bad excuse, really. Way better than *We jumped a fence illegally and then got attacked by cursed coyotes.* Sometimes the truth doesn't sound very truthful. Mom keeps quiet till I've eased myself into the passenger's seat.

"What else was in your wallet?"

I go through the short list: a couple gift cards, about ten bucks in cash. My body aches so much that I can barely think.

She sighs. "Tomorrow we'll have to stop by the security office and then go to the RAPIDS site to get you a new ID card. Meanwhile, make sure you clean those cuts properly."

This is how Mom punishes me. With her tone of voice. When Ryan Daniels almost died falling off my roof in seventh grade. When I convinced David Steir to give me driving lessons with his dad's car in eighth grade.

When Jessie Zhen and I got busted for our traffic cone collection. My friends got slammed with penalties. I got treated to Staff Sergeant Claudia Ventura's disappointment.

Dad's way different. When he's around—which is usually only when Mom's deployed—he'll yell if he's angry. Lecture me. Take away privileges. That's always easier to take.

"Thanks, Mom. I'm sorry."

"Well, I assume this was a learning experience for you."

"Yep." Though I'm not really sure what I've learned. Don't sneak onto cursed abandoned movie sets? That's probably a start.

I text Ahmed. *You get home alright?*

He texts back, *Just under the wire. Sorry I had to rush you guys.*

No problem. We shouldn't have cut it so close.

Of course, we cut it close in a lot of ways. Which I remember when Destiny texts me a few minutes later.

My dad says the arm is broken. Her dad's a flight surgeon. He would know. *So are you convinced?*

I know what she means. Am I convinced the curse is real? Do I believe our bad luck tonight is a sign of something bigger? *Not sure. But at least we're all safe.*

There's a pause before she replies. *For now.*

CHAPTER 6

Edmonds Air Force Base is basically a town with a high-security perimeter. And lots of planes. About twenty thousand people live here—service members and their families. A few hundred of those people go to Edmonds High School right here on the base. That's where Gabby and I are headed Thursday morning, the day after our trip to Sanford's Folly. Mom and I live next door to Gabby's family, so we've started biking to school together. But she might change her mind about that if I keep bringing up the curse.

"For the last time, Alex! There is no curse."

"Look, I'm not coming at this from a superstitious angle, like Destiny. I'm just saying, there's *evidence*. Stuff that doesn't add up logically."

"Losing your wallet doesn't count as a supernatural event."

"But doesn't the curse involve bad luck?"

"Yeah." Her tone could slice an apple in half. "Which is one step up from a curse that says you're going to die someday. Pretty safe bet that people will have bad luck from time to time. I mean, sure, we had some bad luck last night. Ahmed almost missed prayer. You lost your wallet. Destiny hurt her arm. Oh, and I missed my usual phone call with my mom."

Her mom's a professor of film studies in California. Gabby's parents divorced and her dad remarried when she was little. She told me that until her dad got stationed at Edmonds, she and her mom hadn't lived in the same time zone for years. I know those weekly phone calls mean a lot to her. "Sorry," I say.

She shrugs. "My point is, that's not a curse. That's life."

"But those coyotes—"

"Shut *up* about the coyotes! These days, lots of animals are doing things they've never done before. Wandering into the middle of cities. Relaxing in hammocks in people's backyards. Haven't you seen *Mooseland*?"

I'm pretty sure that's a movie only Gabby has seen. And I can tell this conversation is about to get useless. "Fine. I was just curious. Wondering how all the bad-luck rumors got started. Like, if what's-his-name, the megastar, died in a coyote attack, that would be good to know."

"He died of lung cancer," says Gabby acidly. "And yeah, he had plenty of bad luck in his life. But most of it was his own fault. Guy was a first-class son of a—"

A minivan blows past a stop sign right in front of us. We both slam our brakes. Gabby shouts some choice words at the driver.

"See?" I say. "What was *that*?"

"An idiot driver. Grow up."

Time to change the subject. I don't want to push too many of Gabby's buttons. That's how you lose friends. Especially friends you haven't known very long. Which is every friend I've ever had.

So for the rest of the ride to school, I ask her about things she likes to talk about. New movies she's planning to see. Ways her stepsisters have annoyed her lately. The summer program she's applying to at Berkeley, where her mom works. I pretend to forget about the curse.

Until fourth period, which I have with Destiny. While I'm signing her new cast, she whispers, "I did more research on Sanford's Folly last night. I found out some insane stuff."

"Like what?"

"So, the people who worked there. Actors, directors, crew members. Every single one of them had terrible things happen to them. Sometimes during the shoot. And then afterward too. For the rest of their lives." She flicks a stray curl out of her face. Her charm bracelet clinks. "The curse followed them around. Forever."

I draw some squiggles on her cast with my marker. "Can you give me an example?"

"Okay, so there was this director. Martin Feeney. Made lots of famous movies, I guess, back in the day. Filmed a bunch of Westerns at Sanford's Folly. The last one he did there, right before the shoot wrapped, he got *shot*."

My marker freezes mid-squiggle. Didn't see that coming.

Destiny nods. "Yeah. One of the actors brought a real, loaded gun on set. And who would've known? They were filming a Western. Plus it was, like, the sixties, so there probably weren't many gun restrictions back then. Anyway, the actor just walks up Main Street, right in front of the mission, and shoots Feeney point blank."

"Whoa. Why?"

She shrugs. "That's up for debate. I guess the actor had a huge ego and a bad temper."

"Did Feeney die?"

"No, the actor shot him in the shoulder. But Feeney never made another hit movie after that. Plus his wife left him. *And* he was in massive debt when he died."

She raises her eyebrows like this settles the question.

"Well, that could all be coincidence . . ."

"That's only one example."

Before I can respond, our teacher snaps, "Alex, have you finished your art project on Destiny's arm? Or should we wait for you a little longer?"

"Sorry," I say. I dive back to my desk, which is right behind Destiny's.

A minute later, as she's passing a worksheet back to me, she whispers, "You want another example? Look up the actor who shot Feeney."

"Who was it?"

"Earl Morrison."

***

Fifth period. History. We're at the school library, doing research for a project, and I'm way off track. I've been reading up on Earl Morrison.

Destiny's right. His life is like a checklist of disasters. At least after 1961. Up to that point, he seemed to be living the dream. And even when he shot the director, Feeney didn't press charges. But that seems to be the last stroke of good luck Morrison had.

His next film—the one he and Feeney had been finishing up—flopped. Morrison didn't work with Feeney again, but the rest of his movies tanked too. His big affair with Simone DeVray went down in very public flames. Then he fell off a horse while doing a stunt. Paralyzed from the waist down. Instant retirement. Ran for governor of Arizona and lost. His secretary stole a ton of his money. His kids wanted nothing to do with him. And then the lung cancer capped it all off. The whole picture is pretty grim.

I reach the end of the article I've been skimming. An early publicity photo of Morrison fills half my computer screen. It's a classic movie star close-up. Cowboy hat cocked to one side, cigarette clamped between his lips. Yeah, that cigarette would explain the lung cancer . . .

"Alex? How's it going?" My history teacher, Ms. Ruiz, is getting suspicious.

I close the browser tab with the Morrison info. Now I'm back on the school library's home page. "Still looking for reference books," I tell Ms. Ruiz. Better make it convincing. I type something into the catalogue search bar. *Sanford's Folly.*

I don't really expect any results. But one book pops up.

The Atlas of Cursed Places.

What?

Ms. Ruiz is coming around to look at my screen. As fast as I can, I type *Mexican-American War* into the search bar. A new list of books appears. I get to work.

But I can't stop thinking about *The Atlas of Cursed Places.*

That can't possibly be a legit book.

Can it?

CHAPTER 7

It's Tanner Crook who convinces me to find
that book.

Tanner's on the track team with Ahmed
and me. He thinks he's the fastest sprinter.
He'd be right, if Ahmed wasn't around. He'd
also win a team spirit award, if no one else was
on the team.

Ahmed and I are in the guys' locker
room after track practice. We're the last
ones to leave. Except for Tanner, who
passes us on his way out. Usually he has to
rush off to pick up his younger siblings. Not
today, I guess. One more tally for our Bad
Luck column.

I'm sure the world is full of people like Tanner Crook. People who'll say or do anything to get a little attention, to feel a little powerful. I've known people like him at all nine of my schools. Those people have always been outnumbered by people who *aren't* scum. But that doesn't make him any easier for me to tolerate.

"Yo, Osama," Tanner says to Ahmed. "Say hi to your dad and his terrorist friends for me."

I know Ahmed is used to this. I know he prefers to ignore Tanner's comments. And I know that Tanner just likes getting a rise out of people. Still, I can't help snapping, "Real original."

Tanner's already at the end of the row of lockers. But now he turns back. "Oh, you got a problem, Ventura?" He retraces his steps, gets in my face. He's got an unlit cigarette dangling from his mouth. I didn't know he was a smoker. Seems weird for a guy who's so proud of his lung capacity. Maybe it's just part of his macho image. "You got a problem with patriotism?" he snarls.

I *could* say that I'm as patriotic as anybody. And so is my mom. And so's Ahmed, and so's Ahmed's family. We wouldn't be here if we weren't. But Tanner Crook's not interested in hearing that. He's only interested in ticking me off.

And it's working.

"I *said*, you got a problem with patriotism?"

"Nope," I say. "Just with stupidity."

Even though I only met Tanner when school started last month, I know him pretty well. I know what to expect from him. Guys like Tanner are all swagger and no substance.

Which is why I'm *not* expecting the punch.

It splits open my lip and I stagger backward against my locker. Yesterday's bruises scream in protest. I've never actually been punched before. Shoved, yes. Hit in the head with dodgeballs, yes. This is pretty much the same. Except, you know, *way more painful*.

"You just call me stupid, Ventura? Or did I hear you wrong?"

I straighten up. Ahmed says, "Let's go, man." But I'm not listening.

I can taste the blood dripping from my lip. I don't wipe it away. I won't give Tanner the satisfaction. "I don't know, Crook. Did you just say something ignorant and offensive, or did I hear *you* wrong?"

Now he's got me pinned against the lockers. The look in his eyes is beyond intense. It's almost like there's a lit match right behind each pupil. "You're the stupid one, Ventura. Defending your little terrorist friend. It's cute. But he doesn't belong here. This isn't his team. It's *my* team. I'm not letting him take that away from me. Or you."

I'd like to tell him to get a grip. But he does have a grip. On my shirt collar. And it's cutting off my air flow. So talking doesn't seem to be an option for me right now.

"Come on," Ahmed says to Tanner. "Leave him out of it."

Tanner's hold on my shirt loosens. "My pleasure." I can tell he's about to lunge for Ahmed instead.

"Bet your dad will be real proud when he hears about this, Crook." That's the trump card for any military brat. We know that our behavior reflects on our parents. Even Tanner Crook takes that seriously. Not that he'll admit it.

He lets go of my shirt and steps back, smirking. The creepy glow in his eyes seems to fade. He finally takes the stupid unlit cigarette out of his mouth. The way he's looking at the cigarette—it's almost as though he's confused about something. There's an awkward silence as he regains his composure.

"Sure, run home and cry to Mommy," he says. "Have her complain about this."

I sling my backpack over my shoulder and close my locker. "That's my plan." When I was younger, I spent plenty of time keeping quiet about being pushed around. I've outgrown that phase. Tanner's welcome to judge me for it. I don't care.

"Can't prove it was me," he says.

"I'll settle for reasonable suspicion." I salute him before I turn away.

"You ready now?" Ahmed mutters sarcastically as we walk off.

I finally touch my throbbing lip. "Okay, I probably should've ignored him. But I didn't think he'd go all Rambo on me."

"Yeah, that was weird. He's always been all talk. Aside from trying to trip me on the track a few times." He hands me a tissue. "But I don't need you fighting my battles for me," he says quietly.

"It wasn't really a battle," I point out, dabbing at the blood. "It was more like me getting sucker punched."

"Yeah, well." We push through the school's main doors and step outside. "I appreciate you having my back. Seriously. You don't know how much I appreciate that. But I'm not some kind of damsel in distress. I don't like conflict, I don't like stupid risks, but I'm not weak."

"I never thought you were."

He looks at me out of the corner of his eye. "You kind of just did."

I don't know what to say. Maybe I've been looking at Ahmed and seeing a kid I used to be. The play-by-the-rules, scared-of-his-shadow kid I was in third and fourth grade.

And maybe when I look at Gabby I see the fifth-grade overachiever. And in Destiny I see the boundary-pusher I was in middle school. Have I really been getting to know them at all? Or have I just been using them to figure out who *I'm* going to be this time around?

I change the subject. "What's that guy's problem, anyway?"

"Muslims and stupid people, according to him."

I snort softly. "Well, technically, I guess it's terrorists and stupid people. He just happens to be using both those labels incorrectly."

Ahmed smiles. "Assuming you're *not* actually stupid."

That gets a laugh out of me. Still, I'm more shaken up than I'll admit. I think of that look I saw in Tanner's eyes. Destiny would probably call it demonic.

Which gets me thinking about curses again. Tomorrow, I'm going to check out *The Atlas of Cursed Places*.

***

Mom seems distracted when she gets home. She doesn't comment on my lip. I think she assumes the cut is from yesterday. I plan to mention the incident with Tanner after we get my new ID card. That takes forever, but eventually the plastic card is in my hand. On the drive home, I'm about to mention what happened after track practice. But before I get a chance, she tells me her news.

It's the kind of news she gets every couple of years. It kicks me in the teeth every time.

Deployment.

In a few weeks, her squadron will head to Kuwait for six months.

I fiddle with my ID card. It's too dark for me to see it, but I don't need to. I know every piece of information on it. My photo, my fingerprint, every letter and number that marks me as a military dependent.

"Well, I guess there are worse places to be than Kuwait right now," I say. Because I have to say something. This is what Mom does. She loves it. She's proud of it. But I know it's still hard for her. I don't want to make it harder than it has to be.

"True." She pauses. "I'll call your dad tonight."

Mom and Dad aren't divorced. Not even legally separated. Dad just doesn't live with us anymore. He does freelance computer tech work, so he can live anywhere. Except when Mom's deployed. Then he spends an awkward few months with me. I call it freelance parenting.

"It seems early, doesn't it?" I ask. "Your last tour wasn't that long ago."

She shrugs. "It's been about an average amount of time. I just had longer stretches between my last few tours. We got lucky for a while."

Maybe. Or maybe we've suddenly gotten *un*lucky.

CHAPTER 8

About an hour after my mom's announcement, I get a call from Gabby. I'm half-expecting her to say that her dad's squadron is deploying too.

"Ohmygod, Alex, it's my computer!" I've never heard her sound so panicked. And we almost got eaten by wild animals yesterday. "It's totally dead! What do I do?"

"Okay, calm down. When you say 'dead' . . ."

"Well, I was working on my application for the Berkeley summer program, right? And I had a glass of water on my desk. But I swear, Alex, it wasn't anywhere near the laptop. It was all the way at the other end of the desk. But I go to the bathroom and I come back and it's spilled all over the computer and I can't get the cursor to move and I can't type and—"

"All right, first of all, unplug it and turn it off." This is one thing that hasn't changed for me in a few years. My dad's taught me just enough about computers to make me my friends' go-to tech-support guy. I guess some parents do less for their kids.

"I haven't saved my essay yet!"

"Well, do you have it backed up?"

"Backed up how?"

Hmm, not promising. "You know, on a flash drive, online . . ."

"No! It's only saved on this computer. Ohmygod, Alex, what if I lose the essay? The application deadline's this week. I don't have time to redo the whole thing!"

I'm trying not to get annoyed. My mom's about to deploy, and Gabby's freaking out over her laptop? But I remind myself that this Berkeley program is a big deal to her. I take a deep breath. "Just sit tight. I'll be right over. If you're lucky, we just need to dry it out. Then it'll be fine."

I don't say this, but I have my doubts that she'll be lucky.

***

"Maybe it's true," says Gabby as I unscrew her laptop's hard drive. "Maybe the curse *is* real."

I almost laugh. "So murderous coyotes can't convince you. But *this* can?"

"That water couldn't have spilled on its own!"

"Could one of your stepsisters have done it?"

"They're not home. My stepmom took them on a grocery run to the commissary." She chews on a fingernail. "Anyway, I keep thinking about this line from *Sherlock Holmes and the Zombie Thief.* If you rule out what's impossible, whatever's left must be the truth. No matter how unlikely."

"So you don't think the curse is impossible." I gently lift out the hard drive and set it aside to dry. Her battery is already soaking in rice. Next I flip the laptop right side up and detach the keyboard.

"That water spilling the way it did should've been impossible. But it happened. *Something* caused it. Believe me, I'd love to think of another explanation."

Maybe I shouldn't be so surprised by this sudden shift in her outlook. Maybe it's just that I've never seen Gabby change her mind before. I guess I assumed it wasn't something she did.

Now that the keyboard's loose, tiny drops of water sprinkle my fingers. "Well, my mom's getting deployed. So that's another fun coincidence."

She grimaces. "Oh, man. That's a way bigger deal than this." She gestures at the computer. "Sorry."

"No worries. That application matters a lot to you. You have a right to be stressed." I hold up the keyboard. "You'll want to let this sit overnight. Longer would be better. I can help you put it back together after school tomorrow. Then we can see if there's permanent damage."

"Thanks." She pauses. "So what do we do? If there's really a curse, I mean."

"Destiny's the expert on supernatural stuff. I might have a lead, though."

***

As I'm leaving Gabby's place, I get a text from Ahmed. *Got a minute to talk?*

I call him. "What's up?"

"My dad just found out," says Ahmed quietly. "He's getting transferred again. To Florida. We move next month."

I sink down on my front step. "Ah, man." You learn to expect this. You make friends and they move away. You make friends and *you* move away. Rinse, repeat. Like the deployments. It's a script I know by heart. The only permanent thing is how temporary everything is.

"And there's a bonus," Ahmed adds. "Tanner Crook's dad is getting transferred to the same base."

I groan and pick a word that sums up my feelings.

"Yeah." He sighs. "Not that I can't handle it. I mean, we've been at Edmonds together for a year. I can deal. I'd just rather not have to. You know?"

"For sure." Plus, the way Tanner was today . . .

I stare up at the black sky, the pinprick stars. "Listen. Gabby's changed her mind about this curse stuff. Thinks it's worth looking into. Can you meet in the library at lunch tomorrow?"

"Uh, okay."

"Taps" is starting to play. All over the base, speakers project the nightly bugle call into the darkness. Ahmed and I listen to it in silence. Neither of us hangs up.

"Taps" is fifty-nine seconds long. When it's done, the only sound I hear is Ahmed's breathing on the other end of the phone.

I say, "Did you know that the guy who wrote the lyrics to "Taps" actually did three verses?"

"I didn't. I just know the one. *Day is done . . .*"

"Yeah, yeah. *All is well, safely rest,* et cetera. Well, the second one goes like this."

I'm not a great singer but I give it my best shot:

Fading light dims the sight
And a star gems the sky, gleaming bright.
From afar, drawing near,
Falls the night.

"Huh," says Ahmed. "I like it."

"Yeah. For some reason, I've always liked that verse best."

CHAPTER 9

Five minutes after lunch hour starts on Friday, we're all sitting at a table in the library. I set *The Atlas of Cursed Places* in the middle of the table.

"Thought this might help us out."

Destiny grabs it. "Whoa. Awesome! Have you read it yet?"

"Nope. Just grabbed it off the shelf a minute ago."

"Find Arizona," says Gabby.

Destiny gives her a *duh* look. She flips open the atlas and skims through the pages.

"There's got to be an index at the back," Gabby says impatiently.

Destiny sighs. Turns to the back of the book. Runs her finger down the index listings. Flips through the book. "All right. Arizona. Annnnd . . . bingo." She rests her finger on a tiny skull icon right in the middle of the Sonoran Desert, about twenty miles from Tucson. A split-second later, she's flipping pages again.

"Aha. Look, there's an entire entry on Sanford's Folly." She starts reading out loud.

The curse of Sanford's Folly dates to 1961. That year, Hollywood director Martin Feeney filmed Man with the Silver Star *at this well-known Arizona movie set. The film starred African American actor John Willis as US Marshal Cheswell. The character was based on real-life African American lawman Bass Reeves.*

"Whoa," Gabby cuts in. "That must've been super controversial back in 1961. I mean, there are racist idiots freaking out right now about the black main character in *Spy Masters*. I'm going to look up this Willis guy." She starts swiping at her phone screen.

Willis. The name sounds familiar for some reason. I have no idea why.

"Anyway," says Destiny. "Where was I?"

. . . Acclaimed actor Earl Morrison was cast in the supporting role of Sheriff Corley. Morrison was reportedly outraged to be given a secondary role. He demanded that Feeney change the script to make Sheriff Corley the movie's hero. Feeney refused. He reportedly said, "May I be forever cursed if I let your vanity destroy this story. May we all be cursed if I allow that! May this whole place be cursed!"

On the last day of filming, Morrison shot Feeney in the shoulder on set.

"Whaaaaat?" Ahmed jumps in.

"Oh, yeah," I say. "Morrison went full-throttle Wild West. And Feeney didn't even press charges. Crazy, right?"

"Celebrities have gotten away with worse than that," says Gabby, looking up from her phone. "I'm sure the heads of the movie studio told Feeney to drop the whole thing. They wouldn't have wanted their biggest star going to jail."

"Soon to be their biggest *failed* star," notes Destiny. "Thanks to this curse." She keeps reading.

Due to pressure from his studio bosses and his own fear of Morrison, Feeney reworked the film. Most of Willis's scenes were cut. Footage of Morrison from previous films was added. (Morrison refused to work with Feeney again, even on a reshoot.) The original version of the film was never shown or distributed. The recut film was a critical and box-office failure. It also marked the beginning of professional and personal troubles for Feeney, Morrison, and many others involved with the film.

Destiny pauses and gives Gabby a pointed look.

"Gloat later," Gabby says grimly.

"On that note, what happened to Willis?" I ask her.

She glances back at her phone. "Never got another acting job after that movie. Died young. Nothing ultra-dramatic or unusual."

"Sad, though," I say. "I mean, it's hard to feel too sorry for someone like Morrison, since he was a complete jerk. But you have to feel for guys like Willis, who didn't do anything wrong except show up for work."

"And Feeney," says Ahmed. "He was just trying to be true to his artistic vision."

Gabby shoots him an impressed look. Maybe they have more in common than I thought.

"Is there more to the atlas entry?" I ask Destiny.

"Tons more. It goes through a whole long list of other things that went wrong at Sanford's Folly after 1961. Up to and including the fire, when almost every building except the mission burned down. Oh, hey. Listen to this!"

In Feeney's later years, he was often asked about the curse. He told one reporter, "The key to breaking the curse is in the film itself."

Gabby chews thoughtfully on her thumbnail. "An Easter egg. A hint that you'd only notice if you were looking for it."

"Have you seen *Man with the Silver Star*?" I ask Gabby.

She shakes her head. "Never bothered. It's on every list of worst films ever made."

"Well then." I stand up. "Who's up for a Friday movie night?"

CHAPTER 10

Man with the Silver Star is terrible. It makes
no sense. It jumps from scene to scene with
no transition. It randomly inserts clips from
Morrison's other movies—bits of dialogue,
action shots. The goal is to string together
a sequence of events that revolves around
Morrison's character, the sheriff. But you end
up getting distracted by all the inconsistencies.
In one shot Morrison's wearing a hat. In
the next he's not. In the next, he's ten years
younger. Then suddenly he's wearing a
bandana. The dialogue is choppy. The action
sequences have no rhythm. And I completely
lose track of what's supposed to be happening.

Feeney seems to have deleted all the scenes that relate to the movie's specific plot. Probably because John Willis, the Marshal, was in those scenes and Morrison wasn't.

I guess it's kind of cool to see Sanford's Folly in its glory days. On-screen, it looks like a real town. All the buildings on Main Street are in good shape. There's a jail, a hotel, a saloon. And of course the mission. Though each time Morrison throws away a cigarette, I expect everything to go up in smoke. And that's pretty much the most interesting part of this viewing experience.

"Are you picking up on any clues?" I ask halfway through. "Because I'm completely lost."

Gabby shakes her head. "I feel like we're trying to find the stolen money from *Fargo*."

Ahmed presses the spacebar on his laptop to pause the movie. "Well, should we just stop watching, then? It's a really lame movie."

"And the soundtrack is awful," adds Destiny.

"It's not really a movie at all," I point out. "It's like a mashup of Morrison clips. I think the Willis guy has said five lines so far."

Willis. Why does that name sound so familiar? I've been trying to figure it out all night.

"If we stop now, we'll still have no idea how to break the curse," Gabby reminds us.

"Well, maybe we'll be fine," says Ahmed. "Even if we can't break the curse. I mean, aside from the close call with the coyotes, nothing really awful has happened."

"Yet," says Destiny.

That word sinks to my stomach like a rock. My mom's deployment is coming up. What if the curse transfers from me to her? What if my bad luck becomes her bad luck?

And there are smaller fears too. Gabby's application might be gone. She might miss out on her chance at that summer program. Ahmed's about to spend another year or more with a guy who punches people just for kicks. Destiny's arm might not heal right. Those aren't life-and-death stakes, but they're not nothing. They're *life* stakes, at least.

"Okay," I say. "I vote for us to keep watching. We have to at least give this our best shot."

Ahmed sighs and un-pauses the movie.

Forty-five minutes later, Earl Morrison lights one last cigarette. Then there's a shot of a guy on horseback riding away from the camera. I can't tell if this is Morrison, or a stunt rider, or . . .

A voiceover drowns out the music. "Some men are American originals. Some stories will not die. An original will remain, long after the glossy lies and tidy myths fade. An original, if seen by the world, will redeem this land and set us free."

The terrible soundtrack swells, and the credits roll. Ahmed hits *pause* again.

"What. Was. That?" I demand.

Gabby scowls at the screen. "I think that was Feeney's message. That part about redeeming the land and setting us free . . ."

"But how?"

"The *original*," I say. "That's what the voice-over keeps saying!" Electricity shoots through me. "As in the original *movie*. The original version, before it got recut into a Morrison-fest. Maybe we just need to find that original. . . print?"

I look at Gabby to confirm that's the right word. She nods slowly. So does Ahmed.

"Find it," he says, "and share it. Like it says in the last line of the voiceover." He rewinds and plays that part again: *An original, if seen by the world, will redeem this land and set us free.* "If seen by the world," Ahmed repeats. "So I bet we'd have to make the movie available to the public."

"Maybe your mom could help with that, Gabby?" I suggest. "Since she's a film-studies professor?"

"Aren't we getting ahead of ourselves?" says Gabby. I can hear the silent *you idiots* at the end of that sentence. "How exactly are we supposed to find an original version? How do we know it even exists?"

"Wouldn't your mom have some ideas about where to look?" I say.

She throws up her hands. "Even if it *does* exist, do you know how many old film reels are lying around? Like, thousands. People collect them at garage sales. And those people may not even *watch* the films. They may have no idea what they've got. My mom won't be able to find something if it's in a hoarder's storage locker. Or a landfill. Or Martin Feeney's grandchildren's basement."

I can feel something deflate inside me. She's right. We're dealing with a needle in a haystack.

My eyes drift back to Ahmed's laptop screen. The film is paused on the first frame of the credits. Morrison gets top billing, of course. Willis is fifth or sixth on the list.

And out of nowhere, it hits me. *Willis screen test.* The label on one of the old film reels. In the shed at Sanford's Folly. Which reminds me of another labeled reel I saw there.

"I know where it is!"

I can see the label in my head. *MWTSS.* *Man with the Silver Star.*

"The shed. The film reels in the shed. It's one of those."

I look up at the others. Blank stares.

"It's there," I insist. "I saw it. I just didn't know what it was."

Ahmed's eyes widen. Gabby slowly sits up straight. Destiny's hands fly to her mouth.

"You're sure?" Gabby demands.

"Absolutely. The original print is at Sanford's Folly." Then I say what we're all thinking: "We have to go back."

CHAPTER 11

Saturday morning, Gabby picks us up in her family's car. We get a flat tire halfway there, but there's a spare in the trunk. We reach our destination without any other problems.

Destiny has a pair of bolt cutters in her backpack. I use them to cut a slit in the fence. It'd be too risky to scale it again. Plus Destiny can't manage the climb with her cast.

I pull apart the metal mesh. We slip through the gap and start running.

We reach the town. Head up Main Street. No coyotes so far. But we don't slow down. The plan is simple. Get in, get the print, get out, beat the curse. At least I hope it's that simple.

Because once again, this is my idea. If it goes wrong, that's on me. Like so many other plans I've made, with so many other friends I've let down.

We're out of breath by the time we reach the shed. Inside, I head straight for the stacks of old reels. I can't remember where exactly I saw the one with the *MWTSS* label. So we start sorting through the collection as fast as we can.

I'm halfway through a pile when I find it. "Got it!"

"Bravo, Ventura."

That's not a voice I was expecting to hear.

We all spin around.

Tanner Crook stands in the open doorway, casually lighting a cigarette.

"What are you doing here?" I demand.

He grins. Pops the cigarette in his mouth. "Making sure that movie never sees the light of day," he says, taking a puff from his cigarette.

"Are you serious?" says Ahmed. "How do you even *know* about the movie? Were you eavesdropping at the library?"

"I wasn't talking to you, Osama. You think you're better than me? You think you deserve this?"

"Deserve this?" I ask. "What are you talking about?"

He doesn't bother to answer my question. "Hand it over, Ventura."

My hands tighten around the film reel. "You clearly need to get a life, man."

Tanner flicks the ashes off his cigarette, takes a step toward me.

For a split second I wonder whether it matters. If I hand over the reel, I mean. As long as the print's found, does it matter who finds it? Maybe he'll sell it on eBay. Would that count as showing it to the world?

Tanner's close now. Close enough to smell his cigarette breath. Close enough to see the glow behind his eyes. There's a matching glow slowly eating the tip of his cigarette.

Suddenly I'm slammed with an image from the official version of *Man with a Silver Star*. Earl Morrison, casually giving himself lung cancer. Casually destroying the hard work of the people around him.

And that's when I know. Handing this print over to Tanner Crook would be like putting the curse on steroids. Because the curse is inside him, controlling him. It's turned him into an echo of Earl Morrison. Everything he's doing right now has to be the work of the curse.

"I'm not asking again," he says. "Give it to me. Now."

I glance at the others. Gabby and Destiny look furious. Ahmed just locks eyes with me and slowly shakes his head.

Good. We're all on the same page.

"Nah, I don't think so," I say.

Tanner reaches behind him and slams the door shut. To symbolically block our exit, I guess. He takes the cigarette out of his mouth and tosses it away. "You got a prob—"

That's as far as he gets before the wall behind him bursts into flames.

CHAPTER 12

It doesn't make sense, of course. A cigarette shouldn't start such a big fire so quickly. But we're in a cursed fake Western town. If coyotes can form hit squads here, anything's probably possible.

And right now, an entire wall of the shed is going up in flames.

Nobody moves for a couple of seconds. Tanner looks as stunned as the rest of us. That eerie glow in his eyes is gone, snuffed out. Which seems to be the only good news. "Holy—" he starts.

He doesn't finish. Because a spark shoots down from a burning crossbeam, lands on his sleeve, and ignites.

Before we even register it, he's screaming. His whole shirt is burning. Destiny and Ahmed both grab him and throw him to the floor. "Roll!" Ahmed shouts at him while Destiny tries to smother the flames with her good hand. "Roll!"

But the fire's snaking across the floor now, getting closer to us. It's spreading to the other walls too.

I feel the heat creeping along the back of my neck. Getting stronger. Getting closer.

The whole shed is on fire. We're trapped.

Almost.

"The tunnel!" I shout to Gabby, who's closest to the trapdoor.

She leans down and flips the trapdoor open. Destiny and Ahmed drag Tanner over to it and shove his still-blazing body through the hole. As they jump in after him, flames lick at the floorboards under my feet.

Gabby looks at me. I thrust the reel into her hands. "Go! I'm right behind you!"

She hops in. I smell burning plastic. My sneakers.

I'm on the tunnel stairs. I pull the trapdoor shut behind me. I run.

I collide with Gabby, who's having a coughing fit.

A phone light flickers on in the darkness of the tunnel. I hear Tanner moan. But I don't see any flames. So his shirt must be doused by now.

"Everybody alive?" I say hoarsely.

"Seems like it," replies Destiny's voice. "Come on, Crook, on your feet. We're not dragging you the whole way out of here."

We shuffle through the tunnel at a shaky half-run. It seems way longer than it did the other day.

Finally we reach the basement at the other end. I look up at the hole in the ceiling above us. More than ten feet up.

"I'm guessing there's not a ladder down here that none of us noticed before?" says Gabby.

"Probably not," Destiny says. "Fellas? Want to give me a boost?"

Ahmed understands her faster than I do. He kneels down and cups his hands. Destiny rests her foot on top of them. Ahmed looks over at me. "Alex? You with us?"

"Oh. Got it." I get down on one knee, lace my fingers together, and hold them out to Destiny. She slides her other foot into my makeshift stirrup. Her good arm rests on my shoulder.

"Wait a minute," says Gabby. "Shouldn't I go first? Since I have two working arms."

"I'll be fine," Destiny says. "Go ahead, guys." She does love a challenge.

"On three," says Ahmed. "One. Two . . ."

We slowly rise up, trying to move at the same speed, lifting Destiny. When we're almost upright, Destiny takes her arm off my shoulder and reaches toward the ceiling. Now we're standing up straight, and Destiny's got her arm through the hole.

"I'm gonna need the biggest boost you can manage," she says. "I can't grip very well with one arm. If you don't put me over the edge I'll just slide back down."

Gabby lets out an annoyed sigh.

Ahmed nods at me. "On three again."

We heave upward. Her feet rise out of our cupped hands. For a split second her legs dangle above us, flailing. Then she drags herself forward. Three long pulls, and she's clear of the hole.

"Okay!" she shouts down. "Send Gabby next." She scrabbles around to face the hole. She's lying on her stomach, extending her good arm. "I'll help pull her up from here."

Ahmed and I go through the same routine with Gabby. Gabby hands off the reel to Destiny, who sets it aside. Then Destiny grabs Gabby's hand while Ahmed and I push off from below. Once she's clear, I look over at Tanner.

"Let's go, Crook. Unless you want to stay down here."

He moans and staggers toward us.

"Hurry up!" calls Gabby. "I can smell smoke. I think the fire's getting close."

I smell it too. Tanner seems to have set Sanford's Folly ablaze for the second time in its history. I guess I should cut him some slack, since he was possessed by the curse when he did it. But I suspect the curse couldn't have controlled him so easily if he'd been a decent human being.

Tanner's heavier than the girls. He also keeps groaning and can barely stay upright. But with Gabby and Destiny adding their muscle from above us, we manage to get him out. Now it's down to Ahmed and me.

I kneel again. "Here. Climb on my shoulders."

"What about you?" he asks. "How do we get you out once I'm up there?"

I glance up at the others. Gabby looks at Destiny, who has a look of blank panic in her eyes. I realize I might be the only one who's thought this through. I take a deep breath. "You don't."

"What?"

"You leave me behind. You get out of here, and you call 9-1-1. And the fire department shows up and gets me out."

"Whoa, hold on!" says Destiny. "We're not leaving you . . ."

"We'll find a wooden beam," says Ahmed. "Or a metal one. Or something."

"No," I say. "There's not time. Just get out. I'll be fine till the firefighters get here."

"No way!" shouts Gabby.

"We're wasting time," I snap. I turn to Ahmed. "Come on, man. Please."

Ahmed seems to swallow a fistful of protests. He moves behind me and scrambles onto my back. With his knees resting on my shoulders, I slowly stand. I reach up, and he grips my hands to steady himself as we rise. Once I'm upright, he shifts from his knees to his feet, still holding on to my hands for balance. When he's standing on my shoulders, he lets go. I feel his weight whoosh off me. I look up. He's clear of the hole.

Destiny's still lying on her stomach. She stretches her good arm down as far as she can. "Come on, Alex. Just jump and grab my hand. Gabby and Ahmed will hold on to me and we'll pull you up. Like tug of war."

"It's too far." I reach up and jump as high as possible. Our fingertips don't even brush. "See? Not going to work."

Somewhere beyond the hole, Tanner swears loudly. "It's coming! It's coming for us."

Tanner Crook, voice of our doom. Figures.

Gabby whispers something frantically to the other two.

"Guys," I say. "If you don't go *right now*, I'll never forgive you. Seriously."

Ahmed calls down, "Hang in there, Alex!"

And all three of them disappear from view.

I can smell the fire, eating its way through what's left of Sanford's Folly.

I stand in the dark and wait for my luck to run out.

CHAPTER 13

The smoke is starting to fill the room above me. I wonder how long it'll take for it to filter into the basement. Compared to this, the coyote option is starting to seem like a luxurious death.

I'm thinking about texting my mom. Telling her I love her. Telling her I'm sorry. I'm fumbling with my phone when I hear Ahmed's voice.

"Alex! Grab the rope!"

Rope?

I look up. And there it is. A rope, dangling inches from my face.

"Alex, are you okay?" Gabby's voice. Out of breath.

"Yeah, I . . ."

"Well, come on! We don't have all day."

That's Destiny.

I squint toward the hole. Between the smoke upstairs and the darkness down here, I can't even see who's holding the rope. I just know that they're all up there. They're all here for me.

"Where did you get this?"

"The bell tower," Gabby gasps out. "In the mission. That building didn't catch fire. This time or the first time."

So many similarities between this fire and the earlier one. I wonder if that first fire was set by Morrison, or a curse-possessed arsonist, or—

"*Grab the freaking rope, Alex!*" screams Destiny.

I grab it. And I hang on while my three friends haul me up out of the dark.

***

Next order of business: run for our lives.

The fire is consuming Main Street. The good news is that there's not much wood left for it to feed on. The original fire destroyed most flammable materials. So this new blaze has to work a little harder.

But it's definitely making the most of what it finds.

As we charge up Main Street, I pull my shirt over my mouth to block the smoke.

"Where's Tanner?" I gasp.

"We dumped him at the fence," says Destiny. She points to Ahmed, then herself. "While Gabby was getting the rope."

"And one of you called 9-1-1, right?"

"One step at a time," says Gabby. She's clutching the film reel to her chest with one hand and the lifesaving rope with the other. I guess she does have a lot of priorities to juggle right now.

At last, we're at the fence. One by one, we slip through the opening I cut earlier. On the other side, Tanner sits slumped against the chain links. He smells pretty strongly of barbecue. And he's still groaning like he's at a zombie audition. I should probably feel sorrier for him. I'll work on that later.

"Okay." Ahmed pulls out his phone and wipes soot from his eyes. "*Now* we call 9-1-1."

Gabby swears quietly. "We are soooo getting arrested for this."

I look from the flames to the reel tucked under Gabby's arm. "Well, who knows? Maybe our luck's about to change."

CHAPTER 14

Two weeks after our brush with a fiery death, we sit in Gabby's apartment. The final scene of the original *Man with the Silver Star* flashes across her family's flat-screen TV. John Willis's character, US Marshal Cheswell, rides off into the sunset. The credits start to roll.

"That was decent," Gabby says. "I mean, not Oscar material. But pretty good."

"*Way* better than the other one," I add. "At least there was a real plot."

"Glad you enjoyed it," says Gabby's mom, Professor Torres. She's visiting from California. After Gabby mailed her the film reel, Professor Torres got the print converted into a digital format. She's writing an article about the movie and dealing with some complicated rights issues I can't really follow. But her goal is to get it more widely distributed. She wants to set up some screenings for the public. Eventually, people might be able to buy their own copies.

For now, the four of us have gotten a private showing.

Professor Torres turns off the TV. "You've rescued a lost piece of film history," she tells us. "Though I wish you'd managed to do it without trespassing."

Nobody's parents were thrilled about that part. But I'm making it up to my mom by keeping all my activities legal for the next year, at least.

"It was Alex's idea," adds Destiny.

"Wow, way to throw me under the bus! I see how it is."

She sticks her tongue out at me, like we're in second grade, and I laugh.

We thank Professor Torres for everything and get ready to head home for the night.

Gabby walks us to the door. We're all quiet until we get out on the front porch, out of her family's earshot.

She clears her throat. "So. What do you think?"

"The soundtrack still annoyed me," says Destiny.

Gabby rolls her eyes. "Not about the movie. About the curse. I mean—do you think it's broken?"

We all chew on that for a minute.

Nothing especially bleak has happened in the past two weeks. Gabby's computer ended up being okay, and she was able to finish her application. Destiny's arm is healing nicely. And Tanner's going to be fine. Besides, as long as he's at the hospital for burn treatments, he isn't able to torment anyone. We've heard a rumor that his family's planning to live off base when they move to Florida. Which means he and Ahmed may not even be going to the same school.

And none of us got charged with arson or even with trespassing. That's a definite win.

Some things won't change, of course. My mom's still going to deploy. My dad's still going to be weirdly semi-around. Ahmed's still going to move.

He's the one who speaks up. "I think the curse knows we've done our best. That should count for something."

It's weird: they still surprise me. Each of them. In the past couple of months, I've really only scratched the surface of who they are. There's probably a lot they don't know about me too. And nobody can pretend we have much in common. But here we are. "Cursed" isn't the word that comes to mind.

"I like that theory," I say.

We stand in silence for another few seconds. Ahmed shifts the strap of his backpack. Destiny scratches at her cast. The charms on her bracelet chime softly. I put my hands in my pockets and look up at the sky. "Taps" will be playing soon.

"Well then," says Ahmed. "See you guys tomorrow."

"Hey," I say, on impulse. "When you move, we'll stay in touch, right?"

I want to believe it. So many times, I've said this to friends. So many times, they've agreed. But it's hard. Even with texting, email, social media. Once you get to a new place, you use all your energy meeting new people. *Becoming* a new person. You don't have time to keep track of the people you left behind.

But I say it anyway. And I mean it. And Ahmed says, "Yeah." And Destiny says, "For sure." Gabby adds, "Definitely." And I can tell. This isn't just for Ahmed. It's a pact among the four of us.

And even if it doesn't turn out the way we hope, this moment is enough. I'll always have it to replay in my head. It's that moment before the credits roll, when the stars of the movie have saved the day, and you can just take a breath and enjoy the company.

ABOUT THE AUTHOR

Vanessa Acton is a writer and editor based in Minneapolis, Minnesota. She enjoys stalking dead people (also known as historical research), drinking too much tea, and taking long walks during her home state's annual three-week thaw.